NECROSIS

By Rayne Havok

Copyright © March 2021

Rayne Havok

All rights reserved

Cover art by: Rayne Havok

This is a work of fiction, if you find any similarities what-so-ever they are coincidental.

No part of this book may be copied or reproduced without prior authorization from the author.

A man's body is found in the park, all leads are pointing to the strip club he'd visited the night before.

Nothing Chief Cunningham can't handle, until the M.E notices some peculiar and irregular signs of decomposition.

And then... the second body.

Warning:

May offend

☺

CHAPTER ONE

JOSH WHITMORE...

I was nominated unanimously to be the bachelor party planner. Now, I know nothing about such things. I've never been, nor do I ever want to be, married. But the other guys need someone to blame, I suppose, for what might transpire during tonight's shenanigans. If wives or girlfriends can point the finger at me for any, or all, things that have gone on tonight, then it saves the rest of them from the doghouse.

    I think on some level they know that I'd be the one to find us the best show in town. And honestly, after weeks of investigating, and even going so far as to ask around about such things, I've found the perfect location, a strip club simply called Vīrya. It boasts the best private rooms and *all* the nudity one can handle.

It's expensive but, for what I've heard happens here, it should be worth every penny.

The heavy, metal entrance door is hidden below street level; if you had not been given directions, you'd probably miss it. Not great for walk in traffic, but it sounds like reputation alone keeps these ladies drenched in cash. I had to book out weeks in advance to get this VIP room, and even then, it was like pulling teeth to get it reserved. So many requirements, at one point, I thought they'd demanded virgin blood for payment.

The neon light above the door says Vīrya in the reddest red neon they could probably find, the rectangular glow creeping through the crack around the door is also red, giving it a sleezy feel that has me more than excited.

The six of us stand patient, following the instructions of invite that state someone would see us in after signaling our arrival. Our excitement building in wait. It doesn't go unnoticed that the rest of them fall-in just behind me, making me lead them inside when it's time. They are desperate to distance themselves from any responsibility for this.

The women they have all involved themselves with have barely let this event happen. We made promises of checking-in with them throughout the night and met their list of demands. The evenings rules were practically put in a written contract before allowing them to participate.

Lies also were told, plenty of lies. For one, they don't know we are coming here, or even that *here* exists. They do know we are going to a strip club though, topless only. We had to divulge that, you can't return to your house without the woman living there knowing you'd been inside a nudie club, even if it was for only a moment—maybe you had to piss, maybe you needed the phone, doesn't matter the length of time. The glitter and smells will alert them every single time and she's instantly yelling above the sound of your excuses.

So, as far as their women know, we are at a respectable gentleman's club. And it's on my friends to keep it from their significant others. The cover story was made and, if all goes as planned, each of them can answer the questions that may arise with the same response, knowing that if one falls, they all fall.

The door opens and a too-large man merely lifts his chin at us. I'm assuming he wants to know if we know what we're doing here.

"I'm Josh Whitmore; we have the bachelor party in a VIP tonight, it's been reserved." I try to sound authoritative, but the size of this man alone has me feeling like a child, looking so far up to see his face that I feel small by comparison. I'm sure his size alone is enough to keep him gainfully employed here.

"No guns or weapons beyond this point, take everything out of your pockets, put your shit in a container, and then walk through single-file." He sounds like he has something thick lodged in his throat, like half a sandwich from lunch, giving him an ogre-like grumble.

After following all his commands, we walk through the door, the light is blinding, red and strobing. It's hard to get anything accomplished when my hands are jumping through space. We all manage to make it without stumbling, then await further instruction.

There is no music in this secondary part of the building, I can hear it thumping in the distance beyond the walls, but this area is quiet enough that no one has to shout to be heard. It makes me wonder if the strobe light is more for the guest's confusion than anything ambiance related.

The security guard ambles his way over to us, looking even more intimidating as he moves about the small room.

"You can touch. But if the girl wants you to stop, you stop."

Pause for dramatic effect while he scans our faces for sinister intentions.

"No rules, other than what the ladies put on you. I hear even one peep about you not following that rule, the consequences will make you wish you hadn't hit puberty yet. Secondly, the deposit was just that, a d-e-p-o-s-i-t," he enunciates each letter. "It in no way means you have paid for your time here tonight. If I hear one word about you being cheapskates, you will leave here broke in more ways than just that one. The girls work hard and deserve to be taken care of."

Another of his signature pauses while he judges whether we've all gotten the message before he continues.

"Most importantly, have a good time, boys. You're in room 104, Tula is yours for the night." He gives us a grin that almost looks like it pains him to use those muscles.

The hallway is dark and long, giving my eyes time to adjust—and appreciate, the lack of strobe.

Passing an open door, I can't help but peek inside, giving my baby ducks a moment to catch up. The large room has a gleaming pole dead center with the most beautiful redhead twirling gracefully around it, fully naked. We pause long enough to catch her finale—which happens to be the best use of a pole I've ever seen.

I lead us deeper into the hall, and when the last of the numbers still isn't ours, we turn the corner down another hallway, each of the doors having a placard for its number. They are in numerical order, but not all numbers are there, it jumps from 97 to 104 and then 217 next to that.

I enter the simple four-digit code I was given at the time of reservation, after hearing a click, I push the door open.

To say I am surprised by what's inside is an understatement by far. I've been places and seen things in my life, traveled to other countries, dabbled in a bit of this-and-that, but I have *never* come across something like this.

The caliber of women this rinky-dink place has acquired is astounding. I thought the red head from the other room was as close as you could get to a ten, but seeing our dancer, the bouncer guy said her name was Tula, makes the ginger a low seven on a good day.

Tula has the darkest black hair I've ever seen, like the vinyl of new record, it is shiny enough to see a reflection in it; her crisp, blue eyes hold mine as I step aside to let the others enter. The heavy door closes behind, leaving us awestruck by what lies in front of us. We stand frozen in time just staring at her.

She is in leather—red leather, stuck tightly to her like skin. Her nipples are exposed through cut-out circles. The matching red boots, high on her thighs, meeting the hem of her skirt, leaving just a hint of skin to see, part of which is the lips of her pussy.

She's tall and long legged, round tities, probably bigger than her waist, bounce youthfully as she approaches us.

I remain frozen like a deer in her headlights, and it takes her pulling me by the arm to get my feet working. She lifts my shirt over my head, flinging it to the couch, and shoves her hand into my pants, grabbing my apparently already hardened cock. I jump, clearing my throat, "Woah."

"Do you want me to stop?" Her mouth brushes my ear and her soft words flutter right to my dick.

"No."

"Come here boys," she says to the ducklings behind me, but they can't move. The second we made it through the door their jaws hit the floor like boat anchors. She walks over to them, and her absence quickly has me wishing I'd come alone tonight. The jiggling of her ample ass makes the sting of her departure easier to handle, it's full and round, and when she bends to take the pants off the groom-to-be, I can practically see inside of her. Both holes staring at me, calling to me to fill them.

I'm the only one in the room with pants still on so she returns, crouching in front of me with her thighs spread apart, Tula makes a slow go of pantsing me.

My dick springs free, taking it in her hand and squeezing the tip, she slides her finger along to collect the stringy bead that has seeped out. She touches it to her tongue then slowly sucks her finger into her mouth.

Fuck.

Gliding up my body until she's pressed against me. "You taste yummy."

CHAPTER TWO

Tula has us all seated on the leather couch. It's horse-shoe shaped with only enough space in the middle to walk through. It leaves the six of us so close together our knees are touching. She stands in the center of us moving from one to the next, teasing and grinding.

She knows what she's doing for sure. I love the one-on-one attention, but as she's paying it to another, she's putting on a show for the rest of us as well, bending and writhing to keep our eyes on her every move.

She continues until I'm almost on the verge of losing it, my head is so dizzy from lust I just want to come.

Almost as though she can hear me beg, Tula takes a glass from the table, drinking the water that fills it, and then walks over to me. Snaking her hand around my throbbing dick, she milks me until I come, placing the cup in such a way that it catches every drop, like an expert extracting snake venom. She tips it back, and I watch as it slowly makes its way to the rim of the glass and into her mouth, she shows it on her tongue before swallowing it.

Moving onto the next of us, this time waiting until they've all deposited into the cup before taking the drink.

Against my better judgment, and forgetting the proper etiquette of when to touch your dick in public, my hand gets to work on getting her another drink. She interrupts my stroking only long enough to straddle my thighs. Spreading her pussy lips with two fingers she points at her glistening slit and says, "Come right here for me."

I do so without touching her, although it's a struggle not to skim across her for just a taste. It seems she's keeping just far enough away to keep that from happening. I shoot my come all over her lower lips, streams of it landing right on target.

She drags her hand across it all and then slowly licks it clean, one finger at a time and then the palm.

Slinking off my lap and kneeling on the rug between us all, she pulls the tight leather skirt up, wearing it like a belt, and then reaches down to slip her fingers into her wet pussy, the other hand pinching an exposed nipple.

The room is thick and humid with heavy breathing, but in the moments between them, the stickiness of her hole can almost be felt.

Nathan, the least likely to do what he does, stands and tugs on his cock. She seems to love that he's been driven to do such a thing and pulls him closer to her open mouth, tongue out, waiting for his deposit.

It happens quickly and not much lands on the target, leaving her with come across her chest. Against the red of the leather, it's too much to handle. Two more of them get up the moment they see it themselves and yank until they've added to the mess.

She orgasms loudly, leaving us all craving a bit more of her.

She stands, looking a little worn out but not any less desirable, if anything, the slutty way she wears the come as a badge of pride makes her all the more.

"I have money for you, Tula," I say, fumbling to find my pants. The others do too, digging out their wallets for cash.

"Thank you, if you have time to stick around, I'll be dancing on the stage for the final show tonight, you're more than welcome to have some drinks and enjoy until closing."

Her voice is sultrier now, filled with lust.

"Oh, for sure we will, thank you."

She expertly fits every last dollar into her balled fists and strolls away through a second door that I hadn't noticed until now.

CHAPTER THREE

We pull ourselves together, only now, realizing what a circle jerk that was.

The giant bouncer stops us before leaving the long hallway, blocking us from entering the large room where Tula will be dancing later and says, "Tula tells me she invited you to stay. Same rules apply, you treat each of these ladies with respect and you pay for their time."

"Got it," I say. So far, everything has been well worth the time and money I've put into this. I have no problem taking out a loan, a second mortgage, or cashing in my nonexistent child's nonexistent college fund, to spend every night here until my dick falls off.

The ogre moves to one side, revealing the doorway for us to enter. We make our way to the stage where a table large enough to accommodate us conveniently sits open.

There are quite a few people here, but all seem to be keeping to themselves and that's fine with me.

A petite blonde walks up to us, her tits making it to the table first, they practically rest on it as she takes our drink order. We give it to her and she walks away, her naked ass jiggling as it follows behind. I realize she's only wearing a small pocket apron around her hips to hold a notepad and pen. Looking around, I see the rest of the ladies are in the same state of undress. Fully naked dress code for everyone here—except the bouncer, thank fuck.

Our order is delivered and we drink up, watching the dancers as they take their turns on the stage. Sitting silent, for the most part, the loud music making it hard to talk even if we wanted to, as the entertainment reaches amazing levels.

Blondie comes back and asks if we want some food. We order, and then eat when it arrives, it's bar food so mostly grease, but it's actually really good. Overall, this place is definitely something to come back to.

Two more rounds of drinks and Tula is finally introduced by the man playing the music tonight. "Your queen is on folks, welcome Tula."

Unlike the other intros of the night, no one claps, everyone in the room stops and focuses on the stage. The music turns into something hypnotic, and after the first glimpse of her, I can't tell you what happens around me, my eyes are locked on her.

To my surprise, she's out of the lusty red leather, which anyone who has seen her in it would think it to be a mistake, but it's not. She's now in a shear white teddy and nothing else. Her dark nipples, and a tattoo snaking around her mid-section, seemingly put there by the gods, are easy to see through the delicate mesh that falls just below her ass and dances across her body like a cool evening breeze as she starts her show.

The base begins to pound harder and her hands remove the delicate fabric from her skin. My breath loges in my throat, heart hammering with the beat, as it pounds in rhythm to her actions.

The absolute perfection of her nakedness is almost too much, the tattoo is a thorny vine of red roses wrapping around her, contouring perfectly along her pale curves. Not another spot or blemish marring her flawless flesh.

The music seems to be made for her, everything she does, every move that's made, has the beat dragging me inside her show.

She's dancing for a room full of people all equally entranced by her, and yet, it feels like it's all for me. She is utterly consuming.

Simultaneously, the stage light goes dark and the music stops before I'm ready for this all to end. The florescent bulbs flicker on around the room, yanking me from bliss. I feel an overwhelming need to sit here another minute to recover, but the crowd around me begins to stand and head for the exit so I know its expected of me as well.

I drag myself up from the chair regretfully, I'd do anything to avoid leaving here.

Once outside, I light a cigarette, taking a deep drag, and then another when it isn't enough to help me out of my muddled euphoria.

"Fuck, Josh, you really know how to throw a bachelor party." The rest of the guys start babbling about what we've just experienced, how 'this was the best thing ever' and other bullshit. I can't interact, my mind is still back there with Tula on stage.

We head for our respective vehicles and say our goodbyes. Confirming the story for the women awaiting back at their homes.

Unable to actually make myself start the car, I watch the others leave one at a time until I'm the last in the lot just staring at the building. The side door pops open and I see someone emerge, it feels like a fucking dream. I know it's her by the way she moves, confirmation comes when she passes under a street lamp.

"Tula," her name is out of my mouth as I fumble to exit the car, locking it only after I realize this isn't the safest place to leave an Audi unsecure.

She turns, but doesn't stop walking until I get close enough for her to see it's me.

She looks so out of place in the real world, wearing jeans and a t-shirt, things that should blend her in, somehow amplifying her perfection. Her hair pulled high on her head in some kind of sloppy mess, not detracting at all from the beauty of her that really shouldn't exist.

"Josh?" she says my name and I can swear, it's followed by a hint of a smile.

Is she happy to see me?

Maybe.

I fucking *hope*.

"You headed home?" I ask, falling in step beside her.

"Yes." This time she does smile and it makes my head explode.

Perfection.

I look around for another car, already knowing there isn't another one around, "You walking?"

"Yes."

"Can I give you a ride?"

"I'd prefer the walk."

"Can I walk with you?"

After a minute, and what looks like some thought, she says that I can walk with her.

"Oh, great," I say, because it's the only words I can think of. I had mentally prepared myself for a slap to the face or a rape whistle, thinking it would be impossible to *actually* be allowed to walk her home but when neither come, I'm struck dumb.

She starts out ahead of me as I sit stunned in the daze of her unexpected permission, and I have to jog to catch up to her, but we keep the same pace after that.

CHAPTER FOUR

"Wake up fucker, we have a DB," I hear Keith's voice crackle over the radio.

Picking it up, I say, "You know what I've said about being appropriate on the police radio."

"Sorry about that, Chief Cunningham, we have a dead body at Fountain Hills Park."

"Does it actually warrant you calling me in the middle of the night?" I try not to sound as annoyed as I am, but I'm probably not doing the best job.

"We thought so, Chief. He's naked from the waist down, sitting on the park bench. No immediate signs of trauma or injuries but something had to kill him."

"I'll be right over." Reluctantly, I pull myself out of bed and head over to the scene.

Finding the correct area in the sprawling park is easy when you simply have to follow the flashing lights. I pull in and jump from the cruiser. Nighttime has never been my favorite, but that's when all the crime happens, so I'm stuck being out on most of them. Fuck delegating to the next in line, they always confer with me anyway, every little fucking thing, so I just do it myself.

True to Keith's statement, there is, in fact, a dead man, unclothed from the waist down, sitting on the bench as if nothing were wrong with him.

"Hey, Bradley." Keith jogs over to me.

"Listen *shithead*, you *have* to call me Chief Cunningham."

My best friend of over twenty years is new to the force and, aside from his forgetfulness when it comes to how to appropriately address me, he really is one of the better applicants recently.

"I apologize, Chief Cunningham," he mocks but continues. "Still no obvious cause of death, we gave him a once-over without touching him while waiting on you or the coroner to get here." Pointing to the direction I'd just come, "Speak of the devil."

The coroner pulls in and marches to the scene, he's an older gentleman that feels as though this is his only purpose in life, so he takes it as seriously as one possibly could.

When he's done working, and the body is loaded into the van, there are still no answers. The detectives are left to survey the scene and collect evidence while I follow the van to the M.E.'s office in hopes of getting some leads or a direction to follow.

Things like this don't happen in my town, and if this is one of those pose-a-person mannequin crimes, well, then I can't have the perp out on the streets for too much longer, or I'll risk catching hell from mother's screaming about how their kids would be traumatized by the lewdness of bodies left littering their precious parks. Oddly, I think it would be the exposed penis, and not the death itself, that would throw them all over the edge.

Keith radios later to tell me they have a hit on the guy's ID. Now that we know who he is, we can start to investigate how he met such a strange ending.

"His license says Josh Whitmore, he's 35. Lives in the burbs, no wife, no kids, got him working at a law firm. I'm trying the contacts in his phone now; I'll keep you updated."

"Thank you, Keith."

Sitting in my office, feet on the desk, ignoring the paperwork I should be doing after being kicked out of the M.E.'s office for hovering, I'm left twiddling my thumbs.

He promised he'd prioritize this case and get to it as soon as possible, but now I'm up too early, with two cups of coffee in me, and too alert and fidgety for a day of sitting-and-waiting.

My head falls to my chest and I leave it there until the phone rings.

"Chief Douche, we got something."

"You're lucky we're not on the radio this time, fuckwad. What is it?" I ask, laughing against my better judgment.

"Friends say he was out with them at a club, seemed a little reluctant to say which club it was, but after some time, we got 'em singing."

"Ok."

"A club called 'Vīrya' it's kind of an underground thing, by appointment and invitation only. It's less than a mile from where he was found, and get this, his Audi is still in the parking lot."

Grabbing my jacket off the back of the chair and snatching my keys off the desk, I say, "I'm on my way, send location."

"Will do, Chief Cunningham, sir."

I can hear the mocking tone but I don't engage with him, I just tuck my phone in my pocket and head out.

***

"Hey, Chief, we got nothing here from what we can see. No blood or signs of foul play. Got Lake in there pulling footage from the CCTV."

"Thank you." I walk further into the area and survey it for myself. True to Smith's rundown; it doesn't appear like anything nefarious happened here. Minus the dead body, and it reverts right back to the town's park.

Lake comes jogging from out of the alley, excitement plastered on his face. He runs to within a foot of me, taking a few seconds to catch his breath before finally saying what's been discovered. "Hey, Chief, so," a few breaths, "looks like he left with someone. He was the last in the parking lot when she came out. They left together. Obviously, no audio available. But they headed in the direction of the park."

"Great. We got ID on the female?"

"Security guard says she owns the place, her name is Tula, no last name he says—just Tula."

"Ok," trying to shake off the Madonna/Cher vibes this woman is after, I say, "Anyone out looking for home security footage? We may get lucky and one of them caught the action."

"Already done, sir. The owner of the house wasn't home, but we have the backyard cam pointed right at the bench, assuming it was actually turned on and not a decoy, I think we got it. We have Higgins parked in front of the house for the home owners return so we can snag it."

"Perfect. Remind me why I had to get out of bed this morning if everything is going so smoothly?"

"Chief, I can't answer that, maybe cuz his nudity was making a lot of people uncomfortable."

"Yea," I mumble, heading back to my office for more coffee.

I call the club when I get to my desk; the person who answers the phone tells me that Tula will be in at 3:00, leaving me four hours to wait, since the man claims no one has her contact information to get her in any earlier for questioning.

I rest my head on the office couch for a bit.

CHAPTER FIVE

My eyes pop open just in time to see the number flick over and the alarm to sound simultaneously—I have a very good internal clock. I make it to the club ten minutes before 3:00. I get pointed in the general direction of this Tula lady's office by a hulking man of few words.

I take in what I can of the place on my way. It's dark, making me rethink if I have the right room. "Hello?" I call out.

She doesn't respond, but her chair swivels and I'm left stunned for a full minute before I can speak. She's topless, which is probably not uncommon around here. It's more the *way* she's topless, as though it's *not* a thing, that's very much making it a thing.

"Tula?"

"That's me," she stands, wearing only a pair of shiny black boots. Not just casually *topless*—she is casually *naked*. I can't help but notice her tattoo, vibrant and red against her skin. She looks like the quintessential 'exotic woman' that my mom would have warned me about if she had existed in this reality. I lose my train of thought, just the sight of her garbles my brain.

Clearing my throat, and hoping my voice will come out normal, I ask again, "Are you Tula?"

"Yes, sir, I'm Tula, as I've already said."

Damn it, she's right. And she knows I'm flustered now.

"Great," I say, putting my hand on the grip of my gun, not that I'll use it, but it shows authority, also, she makes me feel trapped and that's uncomfortable. "Do you know why we're here, Tula?"

"I don't." She takes a rubber band from around her wrist and pulls her hair up into it. The way she moves, it's almost like she's trying to throw me off. The simplicity of the task shouldn't make her body do these things; it's just fucking rude.

"We are here because the car left out in the lot belongs to a dead man found in the park."

She points to the two chairs facing each other and tells me to sit. I do so before I realize I've followed her orders without any hesitation. She makes her way to the other, the closeness leaves our knees almost touching once we're both seated.

She sits back and props her arms onto the rests, waiting for me to continue. "Are you aware that we have you and him on security footage walking away from here together last night?"

She pulls one of her red lips into her mouth and toys with her tongue in agonizingly slow motion. As if hypnotized by it, I'm surprised when she finally answers. "Of course I know that, they are *my* security cameras for the lot."

"Right." I expected her to expound but I see this is going to be a little more... difficult.

"Could you tell me what you did after you two left the area?"

"Yes."

Moments tick by. "Would you please do that for me?" My irritation has a lot to do with the suffocating thickness in the air.

"We walked."

"You don't say. And then what, Miss Tula?" Sarcasm is my second language, but I'm usually not using it at work.

"Would you like me to tell you what happened last night?" She finds a fallen piece of hair and twirls it around her finger absentmindedly.

"Obviously." I'm able to fight my eye roll, but only barely.

"What fun would it be if I answered that for you, instead of you uncovering for yourself? Isn't the puzzle part of the joy of police work?"

"It would help us greatly if you'd just say what happened last night. Did you end up in the park with him?"

"I'm right here; of course I didn't *end* up in the park."

Mouth agape, "Are you kidding me right now?" If she wants to play word games with me then she can fuck off. "You want to come down to the station?"

"I'd prefer not to; I have a busy day today. You could stay and watch though. Would you like that?"

She stands and puts her hands on her chest, toying with her nipples. Before I can think not to, I have both her wrists in my hands. I tell myself it's to stop her from manipulating me, but that doesn't explain why I've shoved her against the wall.

"Oh, Mr. Control. I like that," she teases.

It angers me that she's actually able to get a rise out of me. "I'm not *Mr.* Control, I'm just trying to solve a murder."

"Do you treat all your witnesses like this?"

"You're a whole lotta something, aren't you? Do you usually play games with people until they're so frustrated with you, they snap?"

"No. Not at all. Usually, I play with them differently, and usually, it involves their *dicks*. I play with them until they're balls are begging to release all that come. And then, I eat up every. last. drop."

Tula has come free of my grasp, leaving my body pressed against hers in stasis, due to shock alone.

"What?" I breathe, not really needing her to repeat herself, but it's the only word I know right now.

"Listen, I'm not going to say anything else to you about your case. I will, however, give you a show."

"No." I'd really love a show, but not while working, and seriously, not after knowing she is so manipulative. I'd probably sign over my house and dog by the end of it. Maybe get a second dog and give her that one, too.

Pouty and sad looking, although something tells me not authentically, she says, "That's too bad, I'd love to know what you taste like. Maybe learn how big that cock of yours *really* is."

"Ok, listen." I start, trying my hardest to regain the authority—even if I am lying and fooling only myself. I step back from her and pace the room while making some announcement to her about 'how the law works' and that we must 'respect it or everything else will fall apart'. "Witnesses are supposed to help police." I turn to look at her,

"Unless you're hiding something?" When I see her standing there naked, it doesn't seem the most fitting thing to have said. And her laughter is more proof that I'm totally outta my league here.

"Take my card," handing it to her as I pull the door open, which brings the rush of fresh air my head was begging for, I continue, "call if you grow a conscience."

"Oooo, snarky Mr. Police Man."

"That's chief of police."

Her smile grows larger, and I can see Tula enjoys knowing she's gotten to me. "I'll call you if I need to fill you in on anything, Mr. Chief."

I escape quickly after that. My head is all over the place. I thought being married was a mind fuck. Like, that it took actual *time* to get all twisted up and shit. But she has mastered the mind-fuck with a quickness I've never encountered before, and I'm both irritated, and hard as fuck right now.

CHAPTER SIX

Walking into the station I feel like a lunatic, hell bent on taking down any fucker brave enough to speak to me. Thank fuck no one does before I make it into my office. I find myself feeling a distinct compulsion to knock-one-out so I can think, but I don't want to give that woman the satisfaction of winning, instead, I keep my hands off of myself.

I have to keep busy, so I call Keith. "What do we know?"

"Uh, well, still… nothing."

Slamming down the phone without another word, I begin shuffling the papers on my desk, looking for anything to clear my mind. I decide to head to the coroner's office, maybe unload some of this headache onto someone else.

Michael Kirby is standing over the body with a magnifying glass pressed to his eye and aimed right at the dead man's crotch.

Now, had that been anyone else, I would have made a joke, or possibly worry, but I know he's just thorough, and not a man to joke with, so instead, I ask, "What do we have?" Walking further into the room and grabbing gloves to put on, I come to stand next to him.

"Well," he says, not looking away from the dead man's dick, "at first, I thought it might have been a bruise." Finally looking up at me, he begins his analysis.

"This gentleman presented with no apparent cause for death. Once I got inside, however, I could see he was completely dehydrated, which one would think, takes a good bit of time to die from, but if it's severe enough, the kidneys make you regret it quickly. Most of his organs were, for lack of a better word, raisins."

"Ok," I interrupt, "why do we have the magnifying glass down there then?"

"Well, like I said, I thought there was some bruising, which isn't uncommon, even the most vanilla sexual encounters can sometimes lead to bruising. This was spreading a bit more though, and is confined only to his shaft. I thought taking a closer look would clear it all up, but it hasn't. Not yet, anyway."

"So, would that play a part in the rest of it?"

"Can't say for sure, I swabbed the genitals and have them next on the list for the lab."

"So, nothing definitive just yet?"

"That's right. I'll have my report to you as soon as I get done, if there's anything that needs your attention before then, I'll let you know."

"Thanks, Kirby." I make it all the way to the door before he calls out to me.

"Wasn't gonna say anything, Chief, but you look like shit, you ok?"

"I'm fine." rolling my eyes, "Got a difficult possible witness." I leave it at that, and go.

Knowing the rest of this could take hours, I head home for a shower.

***

Against my better judgment, I dress in casual attire and head to Vīrya, maybe Tula won't have her guard up if I'm there 'unofficially'. And maybe, I just really want to see her tits again.

Checking in with Keith before I walk inside, I learn that the man whose video we were waiting for has come in and will be looked over by the techs now. Happy with the forward momentum, I shut my phone off and let the security guard know that I'm here for the show. He lets me in and directs me to the stage. I don't sit there, though, I keep to the darkened corner to maintain my anonymity for as long as I can.

I have a drink and then stick to water as, one by one, some of the most gorgeous women have their turns on stage. I enjoy the show, while keeping my eyes open for anything suspicious, and also for Tula, who I'm surprised hasn't been around.

It's getting later into the evening and the club is busy, with most of the people parked up toward the stage for a better view.

This place isn't the throwing-bills-on-the-stage kind, instead, there is a machine on the table that you enter your credit card number into that takes care of all that. Like an open tab, it charges for drinks as well.

How fancy.

The announcement for Tula sends a hush around the club, which makes clear the fact that she can control more than only me.

I'd settled in, but become more alert when Tula climbs the steps and appears in a black outfit; skin-tight and flawless. Two-inch-wide black strips wrap around her, like a latex-clad mummy, leaving all the right parts exposed—those being her huge boobs and curvy ass—like an anti-bikini.

Her soft, black hair contrasts against her porcelain-pale skin, simply splashed with the color of her red rose tattoo, peeking through her dark outfit. It's all enough to make you forget to breathe. But upon closer inspection—which I can't help but do—the pink of her pussy lips appear as she swirls around the pole, sending me into a tunnel of vision that leads only to her. She becomes the light at the end, and my only choice is to follow it, follow her.

Add to the seven great wonders of the world: this woman.

She's up there for five minutes before both she and the music suddenly stop.

Silence from the audience.

"I know it's highly unorthodox," she speaks in her normal sultry voice and it carries to the far corners of the room with no problem. "But we have a new guest tonight and I'd like to give him a taste. Hopefully you don't mind. Feel free to leave if you fear it might be too much for you."

I'm curious to see what she's talking about, that is, until the light guiding her along the darkened path between patrons leads her directly over to me.

She locks eyes with me—mine telling her that this isn't going to happen, hers glinting with mischievous plans to ignore me, taking my hand as I try to pull it away. "You wouldn't be scared, would you?" she taunts.

She practically double-dog-dares me to come up with her. And fuck her if I am going to back down.

I let her lead me to the stage, passing people whispering their curiosities, helping only to fuel my own. If this isn't standard procedure, then what the fuck does she have planned for this 'tasting'?

Hoping I can learn more about her through her nonverbal way of speaking, I sit on the stool someone has so kindly set on the stage in her absence, and wait to learn.

She begins with a little lap dance. Grinding and rubbing against me to the beat of the music, I have to assume was chosen specifically for this moment. I keep my eyes on Tula's as much as I can, even though I'd love to look elsewhere. She puts my hands on her body and the smoothness of it intoxicates to levels of drunkenness.

"Are you scared?" her whispered breath sends shivers over my body.

You don't scare me, I tell her with a chuff and a sideways smirk.

I do get a little nervous, however, when her hand goes to my fly. I struggle to keep my eyes, and cock, from bulging out of their respected areas, while attempting to play her game.

Pulling me up from the stool, she presses against me, tugging my pants all the way down to my shoes. I keep eye contact with her as she wraps her warm hand around my very hard and not-at-all embarrassing hard-on. She doesn't seem surprised to know she excites me, and I don't let on that it bothers me that she does.

Tula dances on me while not once losing contact with my dick, it's absolutely maddening not to have a second of reprieve. It feels like she can tell exactly what is happening inside me.

Resting her ass on the stool, my stool, she spreads her legs and pulls me between them. I mentally tell myself that sex would be the line I'd draw, but she keeps her grip on my dick as she leans back, using only her core strength to keep her in position, telling me I'm not the one drawing boundary lines.

Reaching with her other hand, she rubs her pussy. I can smell her arousal instantly, and it hits me hard, like a drug. Her continued milking keeps my hazy-head in the clouds.

Her eyes hood, and I sense that moments like this might be the only time in her life that she lets her guard down. She loves this, being on display, having people watch her—us.

She comes, and her whimpered moans drag me over the edge along with her, I spray across her tummy and up her chest. Not releasing me, she runs her finger through my come and scoops onto her tongue.

A collective gasp is heard from people in the crowd I'd somehow forgotten were still in existence.

Repeatedly, she does it again, keeping her eyes on mine, eating every drop of it, lastly, collecting the drip on the tip of my dick, sucking her finger into her mouth and simulating a blow job.

My dick twitches, and I know she feels it when, in response, she lifts her brow and gives me a tiny smirk.

She relinquishes my semi hard cock and takes a bow, plucking my pants up as she does, walking quickly away from the stage with them. And me—I go after her.

I'm only a few feet behind her when I reach the open door to her office. She's standing with my pants hooked via beltloop onto one of her fingers.

"Thanks," I say, taking them from her.

"Did you like the show?"

"The one I was in, or the other one?" I stumble, trying to get my leg back inside my pants.

"Both."

"It's a really nice place you have here, very beautiful people," I say evasively, not wanting to give her another moment to sexually manipulate me.

"I know, right?"

"What happened last night?" I sneak back into Chief mode, once I've gotten myself tucked into my pants again.

"He wanted to walk me home."

Surprised I've gotten something new from her, I am actually not prepared with a follow up right away. "And then...?"

"And then," shoulder shrug, "he was no longer walking me home."

"Funny."

"Try as you might, Chief, I can't tell you what happened last night to that man."

"Why not?" exasperation is back.

"You wouldn't believe me."

"Try me."

"I just did, and you tasted as good as I had hoped, maybe even better." Her cheeky, cheshire cat grin would bring rise from a dead man, luckily for me, I look away from it before she can.

Heat finds way to my cheeks; a mix of embarrassment and excitement hits me. If this were not a case I was working, I'd have run in here and laid her down. But I'm the chief of police, and there is a way to respectfully conduct oneself in that role.

"We got some footage of the park—the bench we found him on, specifically." I watch to see her reaction, but can't read it.

"Then you already know what happened."

"The techs still have it, but I *will* know by morning."

"Sounds like you should make it an early night then, Chief." She starts unwrapping her leather bindings and I linger longer than actually necessary until I'm able drag myself away. I shut the door behind me for privacy she doesn't seem to require.

I get home and check for the email message I am expecting, and sure enough, there's a video attached to the email.

Great.

I click on it. It's good quality and I'm glad of that. The first couple seconds has nothing but the bench, and I think they may not have queued it up for me, but then there is movement off to the side, which turns out to be two people. I can see unequivocally, that one of them happens to be our very own Tula. She and the vic are going back and forth verbally about something—no audio. But they sit on the bench together.

He reaches for her; it appears he's brushing the hair off her face.

Very original.

She turns her head when he tries to kiss her. Making a move to stand up, it looks like he tugs her back down. I can only see the back of their heads from this, the only angle. So, I can't gauge her reaction, whether she may be doing that coy, flirty thing she does, or something else.

He tries again to kiss her.

A very clear headshake from her.

And then he pounces. His mouth is on hers in what I can clearly see is a fashion she did not authorize.

I'm stumped though when, instead of running away, or struggling more, she gets on top of him. Her hands go around him, and very clearly, begin caressing his body. The next few minutes is all foreplay, touching, groping, kissing.

The real action starts when Tula stands and removes her jeans before expertly tugging his down just like she had mine. Then she quickly mounts him.

She fucks him with an expertise that says this is not her first time on a rodeo bull, and she goes for a whole lot longer than eight seconds.

When finished, she hastily stands and redresses, then simply walks away, waving once as she turns back to the vic before leaving the frame.

I clearly see his hand go up in a farewell of his own, then he runs his hands through his hair, shakes his head like I do when I finally get away from her—like I'm actually able to breathe again, and lastly, rests his head on the back of the bench. Then the video ends, pausing on that frame.

I look at the body of text that was sent along with it, and it reads. *"She's not our guy. He was clearly alive when she left. Although, he doesn't move after that. My report is not back yet, and there's nothing else on the video until the witness calls it in and we show up. Could be heart attack or something."*

"Could be," I say aloud, but there is definitely a mystery surrounding this woman, so I keep my guard up, haunches and all.

CHAPTER SEVEN

Despite my restless sleep, I'm out of the bed early. I go straight to the M.E.'s office without checking in at the station.

"Oh, good, Chief, you saved me a phone call."

"What do we know?"

"So, the genital bruising I was looking at when we last saw each other has blossomed."

Blossomed?!

"I'm sure *you* know what you mean by that, but I sure don't."

"Let me show you." He leads, and I follow him to the refrigerated drawer the vic is in. Lifting the sheet with a wave of his hand, expositing the hideous looking dick.

"It has definitely *blossomed*," I say, shocked by the change.

"It's still confined to his shaft. I can't tell you what would cause this sort of differential decomposition."

"What's that?" I ask, never having heard the term before.

"It basically means that the decomp progression is at different levels of age or advancement. His penis has rotted, let's say, at a much faster rate than the rest of him. And the sample I swabbed of his shaft is full of necrotic skin cells. Too far advanced to be his own. I sent it to DNA and am awaiting the results."

"So, the dead cells aren't his own. Could they be of the woman he had sex with just prior?"

"Absolutely," he adds quickly, "if she were very dead."

"Well, we saw a very *undead* woman and this guy engaged in sexual activity just before his death."

"I have no answer for you, only observational facts."

"Thanks, doc."

"I'll have the lab send over the DNA results when they've finished, I had them put a rush on it."

A quick wave goodbye, and instead of going to the station, I head to Vīrya to make them give me Tula's info. We need to talk.

I needn't bother though, when I find Tula, instead, leaning her ass against my cruiser when I step outside. How she knew which was mine, or even that I'd be here, is beyond me.

Tula walks toward me. How a woman could actually be so beautiful has surpassed my understanding. My brain fills with giddy excitement like some uncontrollable chemical reaction headed straight for my dick, even though I know she's probably not here for me in that way.

"Chief," she catches up to me, stopping me with a hand on my elbow. She wants my attention and, I suppose, I'll give it to her.

"Tula," I say back in the same straightforward tone she's used.

"Has the video come back? If so, we both know that when I left, that man was alive. Right?" A sort of hesitant certainty resides in her eyes.

"We do know that, yes."

"So, you'll be investigating elsewhere now?"

"I suppose I will have to. Why didn't you just tell me what had happened? This all could have been over for you much sooner."

She seems to think for a minute, "I guess, it all comes down to you. Had I said what I'd known all the way in the beginning, we wouldn't have been able to have all these meetings?"

Her face doesn't look like she's joking, but she has to be, so I laugh instead of wondering any longer about it. Sidestepping further inquiry into her statement, I ask, "What was his demeanor when you left?"

"Maybe... spent, if I had to choose a word."

"Why did you have sex with *him*?" Not intending to sound jealous, it comes out exactly that way, and I see she also notices that it has reared its ugly head. "What I meant to say is, I saw him come on a little strong, only to get brushed off, but then you engaged with him anyway. Why?"

"I can't give you an answer for that. I suppose I thought he was a nice guy, until he proved he wasn't a nice guy. Maybe he got what he deserved."

Neither of us moves until the phone ringing inside my pocket breaks the silence. Fumbling, I answer it. "Yea?" Keeping eye contact with her, while trying to read her, only builds more confusion with every passing second.

Dr. Kirby tells me the DNA he submitted is not the vics, which we'd been assuming was the case. He'd had sex before death, and obviously without a condom. The skin cells—the necrotic ones—are not his. And I can guarantee they aren't Tula's; she's very much *not* rotting. I end the call when Kirby has finished. Thanking him for the rush.

"You wouldn't want to give us a sample of your DNA, would you?" I ask Tula.

"I don't think that would prove beneficial to me."

"Didn't think so. Did you two use a condom?"

"If the video doesn't include such information, then it is not for you to know."

"Gee, and here I thought you'd like to clear your name."

"I don't have to; the video has done that for me already. You've said so yourself."

She is quite perplexing. She's been nothing but obtuse and difficult. Even though it doesn't seem to be for the purpose of annoying me, it does.

"I've got to get to work," I say, making my way around her to my vehicle.

"See you later, Chief."

I watch her walk away and then slide in behind a cherry-red convertible sports car that I couldn't afford in this lifetime, driving away with her hair wild and free.

Shaking my head, I make my way to the office.

***

Everyone is busy on other cases for now, the office is a buzz. Having confirmed there was no way Tula had killed the vic, we are left to believe natural causes, and that Dr. Kirby will fill us in on exactly what type when he finds out conclusively. Effectively striking Josh Whitmore's name off the murder board, moving us along to the next—such is the circle of police work.

I can't seem to shake the whole thing, why she'd have sex with him at all being at the number one spot. My mind is walking through all the scenarios, and from what I saw, sex with the man who only seconds earlier had been looking a lot like a rapist, wouldn't have been my guess.

I don't think she's the type to regularly sleep with her clientele. I know that may seem naïve, given she is in a profession where that *actually* happens all the time. And, for fuck sake, she jacked me off in a crowded room. Still, sex doesn't feel like it would be her kind of business transaction.

She seems to know how to work it just fine without sex, as though the 'dangling carrot' that is Tula drives her sales numbers. Now, I could actually be *way* off with that, and she fucks everyone with anything more than a chapstick dick, but my gut tells me otherwise.

I wonder now, if I should try to get her DNA myself.

Collect it with my dick.

I need coffee.

CHAPTER EIGHT

MARK HUGHES...

Life insurance is so fucking cool. My mom had a policy for me with tons of zeros, I probably won't have to work another day in my life.

To celebrate that, I have decided to take my boys to see some sweet ass-and-titties. Word has been getting out about a club where the girls are full on jacking you off on the main stage. I can just imagine what is going down inside the private rooms.

The four of us will definitely be fucking some strippers tonight.

The fat ass bouncer points us to room 104 and we head in.

The black-haired chick inside is so fucking hot. All of us look at each other as if we've hit the jackpot of all lottery wins.

She has a ponytail on each side of her head, a shirt so short it's showing a *lot* of under-boob—and some *over*-boob. A pair of red, barely-there shorts—that are actually crotchless—and thigh high sports socks.

Every college boy's dream girl.

She pops a cherry red sucker out of her mouth. "You boys are cute." Her red tongue licks her lips. "Take your clothes off."

"Isn't that what *you're* supposed to do?" Chad asks.

I give him a jab in his ribs to remind him to watch himself. We don't want to get kicked out before we unload on this tight piece of perfection.

I booked the best girl; I've heard Tula is, hands down, the one to see. And I'm not going to let Chad fuck this up.

"Tula, pardon my friend, please. You'd like us all to get naked?" I mean, seems a bit homo to even me, but you gotta do what you gotta do.

Tula walks past me and grabs Chad's hand, pulling him to the couch and taking his pants off of him without any trouble.

I try not to look at his dick, but the way she's stroking him is actually super hot.

Everyone else scrambles to get their clothes off, I'm last to do it.

"Sit down, boys."

We do as we are told, and in a fucking instant, she has two dicks in her hands. Then the next two, jacking us all off alternatingly, while grinding and sliding against us. She's definitely done this before.

It's almost hotter to watch her with the others; somehow, she makes it a spectacle.

Tula sits between my spread legs and I slip my hands up her shorts to feel her juicy ass. She doesn't stop me.

She takes a dick in each of her hands while my friends stand on either side of her. I watch her expertly jack them off in mere seconds, directing the loads into her mouth, taking every last drop and swallowing it with a look of satisfaction on her face.

Whoa.

Then she swivels around and ends up straddling my thighs, her pussy so close to my raging cock that I can feel the heat.

Stroking me slowly while grinding her ass for her audience, she directs me to come on her pussy, pointing to the cut out slit of her shorts.

"Come right here, baby." After doing what I'm told, she rotates again, reverse cowgirl, pressing herself to my chest, Tula spreads her legs wide and rubs her pussy, pushing my come inside of her and finger-fucking herself. Dillan is standing above her while she jacks him off in the same rhythm that she uses inside her cum-filled pussy.

I reach up her shirt to squeeze a big tit in each hand, massing them together and tugging her nips, she seems to like it enough to moan for me.

They finish at the same time and she eats his come off her hand and then sucks the two fingers that were inside of her, smacking her lips together and licking them hungrily.

I'm hard again and she knows it. I need to be inside of her. Not really caring that it's against that dude's rules, and having ample signs that she is down to fuck, I go for it. Quickly lifting her up and pressing her back against the couch, I have my dick inside of her before she can even try to stop me, I know she wants it.

I see her face when she realizes it, eyes wide, she may not be happy about it, but she doesn't say no, so I fuck her. Hard. Her pussy is so tight and warm, it welcomes my dick to the wettest thing I've ever been inside.

Before I can even attempt to last longer, I feel myself start to come inside of her. I can't make myself pull out. Even if the room were set on fire, I'd never willingly leave this hole before I nutted inside. My dick erupts as if for the first time, I come and come, filling her full, feeding it to her until I'm drained.

Tula wriggles out from underneath me.

Everyone spent, and a little in shock, they dress quickly after she tells us that we should go now. They realize I need help, and redress me, too.

Leaving with one arm draped around Chad, like a drunk man, we exit as instructed.

"Dude you shouldn't have done that. There was no sex allowed. I can't believe you, bro." Chad lectures me and I don't care.

Totally. Fucking. Worth it.

CHAPTER NINE

"Let's go, Chief, sounds like you would be interested in this one." Keith has gotten more appropriate around the station so I don't have to lecture him as much, but it still remains, that no one can seem to do anything without me.

We head out in our own respective cruisers and he fills me in when we arrive at the scene.

"Grandmother called it in. Says she couldn't rouse her grandson for breakfast. Looks like he died sometime during the night. He was a healthy, young male that came up dead without explanation. You told me to bring you in on any such calls so here we are."

Walking into the basement through a private entrance, we see a young, twenty-something, man dead in his bed, wearing what appears to be the clothing he had on last night.

Could be an OD.

"How far out is Dr. Kirby?" I ask anyone who knows the answer.

From Keith, "He's got a three-minute ETA."

"What do we know for sure?"

Keith again, "He got in late last night. He'd been out with his friends. Edith, the grandmother, heard him arrive at about midnight and then nothing for the rest of the night. Waited until 10 a.m. to try to get him up for breakfast. Messed her up pretty bad, dispatch said she could barely get the words out on her 911 call."

"No vomit or foam around his mouth or nose, he doesn't smell overly alcoholic, no track marks." I look around, without disturbing anything. "Do we know where he was last night?"

"Edith says he and three of his friends went to a club. Her words exactly—a filthy, nude, dance club."

I instantly think of Tula. Trying to shake that woman from my head has been... difficult, to say the least.

"We know which club?"

"She didn't know, all her info came from overhearing the men talking, but I *was* able to get the numbers for the friends he was out with."

"Text the numbers to me," I tell Keith.

He does it then, sending a vibration inside my pocket as I continue to look around.

"Dr. Kirby, good to see you," I say when I see him peek inside the room.

The sea of uniforms part so he can get inside, instantly getting into investigation mode.

"Alright, lets clear this out, the rooms too small for us all," he barks, waving his hand to shoo us off.

Once outside, I make the call to the first of the vic's friends. After speaking with him, I have all the information I need.

"I am heading over to Vīrya, seems we may have to talk to Tula again." I try to keep the electric sensation from reaching my voice.

"The stripper from the park-bench-guy?" Keith asks.

"The one and only. Tell Kirby to keep me apprised."

"You got it," Keith says, staying behind to keep everything as orderly as it could be.

***

I get past the security guard quickly enough after he tells me Tula happens to be here at this early hour, but that I may have to wait until she's done.

I see her instantly; her presence drags my eyes toward her and drops my jaw. Time spent living in my memory had dulled her beauty, there is no justice done for her inside a mind, reality brightens her vibrantly.

I watch her unashamed while she dances across the stage.

Giant butterfly wings attached to her back in all the brightest colors, a small circle covering both of her nipples, and nothing on the bottom but glitter, she looks like a fucking fairy.

She gets through the dance twice before exiting the stage and bounding straight for me.

"Hello, Chief," she says like we're old friends happy to reconnect.

"Tula," I say sternly. Hoping it comes across with authority, instead of the frustration I attribute to being so attracted to her.

"What brings you in?"

I wait until we get into her office before answering her.

"I have a case."

"Could you help me with the wings?" She turns her back to me, leaving me out on a limb to figure out the correct way to remove them.

Hanging them up, she pulls the small, sticky circles off, puckering her nipples, and then finally gives me her attention.

Tula makes no attempt to cover up, she just stands with her hands splayed on her hips, picture perfect in her nakedness.

"It appears that this was the last place he was seen alive."

"I doubt that." There is a hint of flirting.

"Friends of his say he was here last night. Names Mark. Ring a bell?"

"I did have a party for a Mark Hughes last night, three others were with him. But they took him out of here very alive, a little drunk, but alive."

"Yea, but don't you think it's strange. We have two men, no apparent COD, both last seen with you."

"Oh, no, I don't think that's strange. Coincidental, possibly, but strange, not at all. People tend to come here for a wild night, wild can sometimes lead to death."

Somehow, we've gotten very close. I only realize it was my doing when I look around to find *my* position has changed.

"I just came here to see if you'd be willing to give an account of last night."

"I am not."

"Do you have video of the private room?"

"No, those rooms, like this one, are *private*." She closes the last of the gap, taking the final step toward me, she presses her body against mine. She didn't use to be this brazen. "You could have called, you know, instead of coming here."

I only now realize that.

"Do you have any evidence that *actually* led you here?" Her hands come up and run through my hair and down the back of my neck.

"Not yet."

"But you thought you should rush right over, with not much more than a crumb of reason, to question me?"

I can only nod. Her hands are all over me now, avoiding only one area, the area screaming at her to touch.

It dawns on that this was foolish and could have been handled better with a more level head. That my subconscious tricked me into thinking that seeing her was necessary for the case, when really, the case is the furthest thing from my mind now.

"It really is nice to see you, Chief. Is there anything else I can do for you?"

My mind rushes into the gutter, splashing about in the filth. I think of many things I'd like her to do for me—to me, but I shake my head instead.

Her hand covers my fly as if I summoned it there with a granted wish.

"Can I help you with this?" Without waiting for an answer, she pulls my hard cock from my open zipper hole and grips it firmly.

I can't tell her to stop, my voice no longer works, and my body belongs to her.

She presses herself against me, bringing me so close to the edge of coming that I ache. Getting on her knees, sucking the length of my dick into her throat until her lips are kissing my pubes, she forces my come out in jolts and swallows every bit.

Only when her mouth is gone do I realize what's just happened. I'd been so accustomed to her face in my fantasies it's almost as if this could have been one. The only think telling me it wasn't is the sensation unlike anything else, tingling inside my balls.

Feeling exposed, I tuck myself back into my pants.

"Did you like my butterfly dance?" she asks, running her pinky over her bottom lip to smooth her lipstick out, there's a vivacity in her eyes I'd not seen before.

I don't even know what she's talking about at first. "Oh yes." Cough. Cough. "It was great."

She slips a t-shirt on. It'd been right next to her, and I feel as though she could have done that earlier.

She's still so fucking sexy, it really doesn't matter what she's in, or not in. She's just fucking *sex*.

"I'm glad you came," she says with a toying smirk.

The double entendre is not lost on me.

"If I need anything else from you, I'll let you know," I say, meaning about the case, but I don't think I say it that way.

"I look forward to it." Her tongue wets her lips, reminding me what they feel like on my skin.

I leave, it takes an extremely focused effort to fight against the pull to stay. I know somewhere in the back of my mind that she's getting harder to resist and that it's dangerous.

I pull my phone out and connect to Kirby. "Hey Doc, could you do me a favor?"

"Absolutely, Chief. What is it?"

"Could I have you check for those necrotic cells on the vic and expedite DNA results, first thing?"

"You thinking he has a link to the unsolved from a few months ago?"

"I think I am thinking that."

"You got it; I'll make time to do that as soon as I can."

"Great, thank you."

I climb into the cruiser, taking an extra-long look in the direction of the club. Although hidden from my sight, I beg it to tell me what the fuck is going on with Tula.

***

"You got something for me?" I ask Kirby after answering his call. It feels like I've been waiting for this all day, but he's actually made good time on my request.

"Well, I've only done a cursory exam, but I can already see the petechial pattern around the vic's shaft. I've done a swab and taken the sample of skin to be compared to the last. I'll let you know the outcome, could be hours though, the lab is backed up."

"Got it, thanks."

So, there *is* a direct link here between these two guys. Unclear whether Tula had sex with the second, but if I was a betting man, I'd say it's exactly what happened. What is it about sex with her that would lead to the bruising though? I mean, could she have Kung Fu grip down there? And even that doesn't answer the necrotic cells. I'd wager they'll be present here too.

***

By the end of day, I still haven't gotten anything else from Dr. Kirby. I need answers. I need to understand this. I know Tula won't disclose anything, but I feel like I won't get anything from her unless I *try*. And there's still a small part of me that can't stop thinking about the fucking butterfly dance she was practicing and it's driving me crazy.

Pulling up to Vīrya, sparing only a few minutes before she closes down the place with her show, I'm able to sneak in, and hopefully, keep my being here a secret for now.

Keeping to the shadows, my head down, I order a drink from the table's tablet and it arrives shortly after by a beautiful set of identical twins. One in gold boots, the other in silver, and that's all.

Fuck me.

"Thank you," I say to them, and in unison, they welcome me to the event.

Sipping slowly, I watch the performer on the stage. She's also in wings, jade colored to go with her auburn red hair, her set much smaller than Tula's, although, still making quite a statement. She's an expert on the poll and it keeps my mind from reeling for a moment.

My mind stops completely when Tula appears on the stage for the finale. I thought I'd seen her at her best during rehearsal. But I'm almost floored by her right now. She is fucking *stunning*.

She makes everything else fall away while she's up there. The room stops and it's just her and this twinkling music that pairs perfectly to her routine.

When it's over, Tula leaves the stage, walking through the crowd. She takes me by the hand, leading the way to her office. I feel a bit of pride having made every person in that room jealous that she has chosen me, even if I'm still unclear what the motivating factor for that choice might have been.

Once inside, I hear her engage the door lock, surprising me, since privacy has never been her thing before. "I don't suppose you're going to let this go, are you?" Her voice is somber.

"I don't even know what letting go would mean."

"Could I confide in you?" She hasn't turned from the door, her back is to me, giant wings still attached.

"I suppose I could be open to listening."

She finally turns, there are tears flooding her eyes, and fuck if they don't enhance her beauty even further. My cock quickly swells, leaking a few of its own tears.

She gestures to me for help out of her wings and I oblige. She indicates the two chairs, waiting for me to sit before she does.

"I told them no," she says, abruptly.

"No to sex?"

"Yes. I was *very* clear that sex was not permitted."

"Ok. So, there *was* a sexual altercation between you and Mark Hughes?"

She nods her head, "He was *inside* of me before I could stop him."

"Not that I have any room to ask this, but why not call security?"

"It was too late for him by then."

"Too late how? What happened to him?"

"I want to tell you this, just so you can get the understanding you *obviously* need. But I will not let you do anything about it. If I feel threatened in any way, I will have to act."

I'm sure she can see me puff up a little from the threat. "How about you tell me what happened and I'll judge whether or not I take that information to the system that governs this country."

"You wouldn't make it that far."

She is smiling, but her words don't sound like a joke.

"So, you want to tell me something, and I have to keep it a secret, or you're going to kill me?"

"Right." The smile is gone now.

"And what if I just took you to the station and had you booked on threatening an officer?"'

"I suppose I wouldn't kill you for that, but I wouldn't go with you."

I give up; I suppose I can cross the bridge when the time comes, but right now, I'd really like to hear what the fuck is actually happening around here. "Go ahead, Tula. I'm listening.

CHAPTER TEN

TULA...

His posture is not at all what I need right now. He's rigid and rough, very agitated at having his power threatened. I like him much more when his body warms, the fluidity of him when he opens to me is refreshing. I understand now is not the time to gratify him, but my senses remind me of the taste of his pleasure.

He keeps his eyes on mine instead of letting them roam as they usually do.

Too bad.

I start, "Do you believe in any kind of ancient lore?"

"Like a vampire?" he rolls his eyes. "Are you about to tell me you're a vampire?"

"No, older"

"Like Medusa or something?"

"Well, I clearly don't have snake hair, but yes, ancient tales like that. Do you believe that they are real?"

Deadpan, "Not at all."

"Do you at least believe that things written about them could stem from somewhere?"

"Imagination," he says, definitively.

"You assume that before there were people, there was just... nothing?"

"I guess, maybe amoeba." He shrugs.

He is not taking this as seriously as I'd hoped, but he is patiently waiting for me to get somewhere, so I try to break it to him. "Well, I can say that there was—and are, things older than humans in existence."

"Oh, there *are*, like in today's world?" he mocks me with his tone.

"Yes, I know of quite a few."

His eyes squint like he's laughing at me. I feel him loosen up, now that he thinks I'm talking crazy, his walls are coming down just a bit.

"Chief Cunningham, tell me your name."

"Bradley."

"Bradley. I like that much better."

"I'm sure you do; it takes my authority away for you."

This time I smirk. "Bradley, I just want to tell you something, maybe more as a friend than for your inquiry."

"Fine, friends we are." Settling into the chair, he lightens up a bit more, even if just for show.

"I'm one of those that are older than humans."

A full laugh. "Oh, baby, I definitely think you're out of this world hot, but I'm not going to go as far as *before* this world hot."

"But I am."

"Tula, are you trying to tell me you're some succubus, feeding on the souls of men?"

The fact that he jumped right to that is funny. "I'm much older than succubae."

"Of course you are, but you don't look a day over werewolf."

"Werewolves aren't real."

"Of course not," he mocks me.

"But Medusa was real?" he asks half-heartedly.

"Yes, and she was actually much more personable than people think."

"I'm what the succubus lore comes from. I'm the first woman of the world. The first everything, I'm the Earth's balance."

I think I really lose him there. Just blink after blink from him.

"There is nothing older than me."

Blink

Blink

"I feed off of life, but not in the way you may think, not by sucking out souls, but by eating the very basic form of life. The beginning of life."

Still nothing.

"After many years, I learned how to control how much I take, so I don't have to kill, although, my purpose is just that. I learned to use my hands, and eat in moderation.

"Something happens when its extracted vaginally, one of the ways I'm intended to eat. There is a force within me that is triggered by that energy. Once that substance is detected, the force will drain every drop within its reach and leave behind death in its place."

"So, your vagina has suction." His eyes bulge. This intrigues him.

"I do know what happens to the men after I engage with them, so I can assume you've seen it too. The death spreads from the point of contact, slowly at first, but soon, it effects all living tissue."

He nods. "That's from you having sex with them?"

"Well, the two you've found were not sex, they were both told no. But yes, that is what happens when a man has contact with me. To completion." I add.

"Ok."

"There are many ways I can feed off humans, not only sperm, it happens to be my preference, so I generally don't use the alternatives. I have this place, my club, and I've had others. They have afforded me all the life I need in order to maintain."

"Just to be clear, when you say life, you are talking about come."

"Absolutely, it has everything in it to create and build. It's essential to everything. The start of it all."

"What if you were to just try a sandwich?"

"Will you be as old as me, ever, sandwich eater?"

He laughs.

"Are you likely to be able to keep this a secret, Bradley?"

"There's definitely no one I could tell this to and keep my job or reputation."

"Great." I stand and pull him to his feet, taller than me, but not by too much in my healed-boots. I look into his eyes while he makes no move to leave. "I could show you."

"Show me what?"

"How it feels to be inside of me."

***

My dick swells, I try to ignore it, but god damn if it won't shut up. "You could show me how your pussy feels and then I'd end up like the dead men."

"We can stop before it's too late." Tula has my pants down lightning quick, her hand around my throbbing dick and I can't say anything else. I don't care if this crazy chick might fuck me to death, I'm unable to deny her. She's already jerked me off—and in my police uniform at that. Who am I to try and be better now? Especially when she looks very eager to show me.

"Show me."

"You'll have to stop before you come."

"Ok." I'm trying to keep that in my mind as she climbs on top of my lap after pushing me back into the chair.

I nearly come out of my seat when I feel the slick pull of her hole. Inching down so slowly, the milking tightness alone will have me empty any second. It's like I suddenly have a thousand times the sensation along my dick. Couple that with the throbbing heat, and she has me on the cusp of exploding only seconds. She's not even completed a full up and down circuit yet.

When I come to—which is not exaggerated—I realize I've come inside of her mouth, she's had the wherewithal to remove my dick just in time.

Climbing into my lap like a cuddly cat, she caresses my body while I'm left twitching and coming-down from literally—and in no way exaggerated—the best thing I've ever felt.

It dawns on me a moment later, that if she was telling the truth, and her pussy does kill men, which I can *absolutely* believe now, I'd just let her do it with no qualms, and would probably have begged for it, essentially putting my life in her hands. I'm an idiot. Or maybe, all these other men who haven't had a chance to be inside Tula are the idiots. Wouldn't be the worst way to go.

"I told you," she says when she sees I'm back.

"I'm not going to *die* now, am I?" I have to ask.

"No."

"Good."

***

Trying as I might, I am unable to get Tula out of my mind, and more directly, her magical pussy.

I've had sex with plenty of women, young, old—not old-old, but older—all varieties, and I can honestly say that I have *never* felt something like that before, sadly, as soon as the feeling of it dissolved, I was aching for it again. It may be the most addictive thing I've ever experienced, and I'm not prone to additive behavior. So, the uneasy and anxious feeling I'm having, is really off putting.

Kirby informed me that this latest vic, like the last, shared all the same symptoms around the genitals, including the necrotic skin cells which share matching DNA markers. It's been put into the database, searching for others, assuming that in all these years, there could be more. I can't help but check every couple of minutes to make sure my dick isn't showing any signs of bruising. Relief hits each time it remains normal.

After doing what needed to be done around the station, I decide that a visit with Tula would be the best thing for me to continue being productive.

Vīrya doesn't have its lights on at this time in the afternoon, the doors open at 7pm, but Tula is usually around by 3:00 doing rehearsals, so I show up at 1:15 and hope for the best.

The big security guy at the door, who must stand there all day, lets me in and tells me she's in her office.

I find her messing with her hair, she's curling it, I guess.

"Bradley, I was kind of hoping I'd see you." Her voice is soft and warm, unlike the other times, where I could mostly hear hesitant obstruction.

She stands and walks over to me, only a tiny silk robe covering her.

"We got results back from the lab, I'm sure you know what they say."

"I can assume." She looks away a little nervous. "Are you here to arrest me?"

"Not yet."

She looks me in the face, trying to read me. *I don't even know what I'm going to do, what I can do, so, I am positive she can't get anything from my expression as she tries to read it.*

"I can't stop thinking about what we did."

She smiles shyly. "Did you like it?"

Her demeanor has always struck me as a strong woman, in full control, but the submissiveness that's happening now is nice too. Kinda makes me want to take care of her. "I'm sure you know I liked it." I walk up to her and tug the tie to the robe and it slides down her shoulders and piles on the floor at her feet.

Pulling her into me, I kiss her mouth, and a hint of cherry hits my taste buds. She tastes just like I thought she would and it drives me wild. Her mouth and tongue work as expertly as her pussy. She was born for this shit.

Her hand inches it's way toward my dick as it stands waiting for her like a kid at a bus stop. I steer us back to the vanity and rest her ass on it, spreading her legs wide.

"You have to remember to pull out."

I push into her slowly, letting my dick savor it all. Every part of her warm hole has things going on, tiny suction, and massaging like the muscles of a snake. There may even be a vibration much like a cat purr, but that could also be my heart speeding with exhilaration. I don't move once inside her, all the stimulation I need is there naturally.

I don't think it could possibly get any better, but then I feel her squeeze, surprising me. "You like that?"

I nod, eyes practically rolling around in my head.

She puts her hands on my hips and pushes, then pulls me into her, only the subtlest movement, but it throws me over the edge. I panic for a second as I feel myself start to come but she has taken my dick into her hand just in time and my release is safely on her thigh.

My shaky legs betray me, leaving my ass barely landing on a chair, just enough of it there to catch me or I would have hit the floor.

Tula quickly eats my come. It is actually pretty hot, even though it's for nutrition, or whatever.

"How much do you actually *need* to eat?" I ask, curiously mostly.

"I don't have an answer for that. Whatever I can, I suppose."

I, myself, think I would probably just die if I were forced to consume any bodily fluid for survival. "And you've always chosen to eat," I point at my dick, "this."

"I just prefer it—to the alternative."

"Which is?"

"Unimportant, it only matters that I don't have to use alternatives. I maintain this way, and have, as long as humans have been upright."

I don't think she's being evasive, but I do feel as though she may not divulge this much to people generally, and might be reserved because of that. "Do you have to eat every day?"

"Multiple times, yes."

"Or what? What will happen if you don't?"

"Mostly, I become weak, my cells are ever dying, and in order to produce new ones, I need to consume. If I don't," she seems to think about how to say the rest. "I rot."

"Would you die? You said you were older than anything."

"I *can* die. It would take a very long time, longer than your typical life cycle to do so though, if it were simply from starvation."

"Are there others?"

"There are."

"A lot?"

"There are enough."

"Can you reproduce?"

"No. That's not for us. We are from the time of the earth's creation."

"Male and female?"

"No, our purpose is best suited in the female form."

"Why is that?" My detective side is making this seem more like an inquisition now, and I can see her pulling back.

"I will say, our purpose is fulfilled best in this form. While we are alluring, it's only a byproduct, we must be approachable so we can eat."

"One more question."

Her smile tells me she is relieved we've come to the end.

"When was the last time you had a man like me? Like an intentional sex partner."

She smiles. "You know it's been so infrequent that I can't even remember. So very long."

"Does it feel good for you?"

"Yes, it is the reason I am here—to consume. For you it feels good because your reason is to create, though we are opposites we are also the same."

"Could we do it one more time before I get back to work?" That itchy anxiousness is back. As soon as I thought about having to leave her behind it kicked in.

"Absolutely."

CHAPTER ELEVEN

I've spent a week away. A full seven days of trying to forget what she does to me—like mind control, by way of my cock.

I took some days away from the office and shut off my phone. My plan had been to find a way to forget about Tula's allure and be able to function normally as an officer of the law without my head being stuck in the clouds dreaming about my dick being stuck in her.

I believe I may have come up with the best solution to achieve my mission, and after a few days of hard work, I am ready to see if I'm right.

Tonight, I'm going to Vīrya, and it will be the last time I show my face there. I can't be on their security camera every day, nor can I be seen by the big man at the door, especially when the link between this place—Tula more precisely, and the dead men with rotting crotches, becomes more apparent to the rest of the department. And god forbid we add another stiff to the pile, it would surely lead to an IA investigation. They'd have my head, or at the very least, my badge, either would mean the end for me.

Everything is ready, I've done my best to make sure Tula can remain safe, stay out of prison, and ensure I can still satisfy my need for her.

***

I show up just in time to watch her perform. God, she is too much. Just the sight of her now sends my dick into a frenzy, a magnetic tug so hard I can feel it ache inside my balls.

I sit, impatiently waiting for her show to be over so I can finally get some time alone with her.

There is a part of me that wishes she'd never let me inside of her. That I could go back to the time when I didn't know such a sensation existed. That sex was just a good feeling, with a great release. But now that I know it's a fucking mind-altering thing that sends my entire body into goosebumps, warping every interaction I've had before, and inevitably after, into some boring task, she's essentially castrated me.

What would be the purpose for my cock, for me, after her? There would be none.

This is my new life. Life after Tula. This is the new me?

Not for long.

I walk into her office just as the music stops. She meets me inside a few minutes later.

Fishnet stockings and devil horns are all she's got on. Walking toward me, I finally feel a little more relaxed, knowing I can get a release.

Unzipping my dick from my pants and kicking them to the side, I grab her wrist and move her hand to it. She squeezes and rubs me. The tension begins to fall away.

"I really liked the show," I say, remembering that I should be polite. I did like the show, I always enjoy her performances, so it's not a lie. But this is the performance I really need.

"I'm glad, Bradley."

I put my hand between her legs and feel her warm pussy. She moans.

"I need to be inside of you."

"I can see that."

Lifting her into my arms, my dick slides into her before I get us over to her vanity. Ecstasy overwhelms me and I almost drop her, but we make it in time to rest her on top of it. I try something I haven't yet. I move inside of her and actually fuck her like I normally would, adding friction to the cocktail.

I get three deep thrusts before I need to stop and pull out. She watches as I jack myself off onto her tits. I needed to know that I'd be able to do that, to pull out. Having that confirmed, I know she doesn't own me and my plan has hope for success.

She wipes up my come then sucks her fingers clean while I watch.

Pulling my pants on, I say, "The case is getting closer to you."

"Is there anything you can do?" She appears uneasy, yet somehow hopeful that she can be safe with me.

"Not without showing my hand, I'm only a cog in the machine, Tula. If I start going around messing with things I've never been involved in all of a sudden, then someone, or more likely, many someone's, will know something is going on."

"I understand."

"I do want to help you."

"How would you be able to?"

"Well, I could take you to my house to lay low. Make everyone believe that you had just run off. I could keep you off the grind, so you wouldn't actually *have* to leave."

"And why shouldn't I just go off-grid, *actually* take off and start over somewhere else? It's not hard, I've done it before—many times... all the time."

"Do you want to do that again?" I can feel the real question showing itself.

"Are you asking if I want to leave you behind?"

"I think I *am* asking that."

"I absolutely do *not* want that."

"Good. I don't want it either."

"What is the time frame?"

"I think, honestly, the earlier, the better."

"So, like, now? Is that why you're here tonight?"

"Yes."

"Can I hear a run-down of what you're thinking, what the plan you've formulated for me might be?"

"Of course, here's what I have so far." I sit on the chair and call her over to me, resting her on top of my lap. "I am going to leave in my car, so I can be seen on the footage leaving. I'll park on the east side of the building where I'll help you load whatever it is you may need from here. And you, of course." I kiss her forehead and then ask, "Would you need anything from your house?"

"I have everything I'll ever need secured."

"Ok. Then you'll come to my house, they would never look for you there, and if by chance they do, I've got contingency plans."

"Ok." She bites her bottom lip; making it seem like she's apprehensive about it all, but the spark her eyes tell me of her trust in me.

"Are you sure you'd want this? You have to be a hundred percent invested. You can't show up again in a few weeks, they'll think, for sure, you'd been up to no good."

"I'm sure. I don't want to have to live apart from you, I've grown to like you very much. You've kept my secret and I trust you to do what's best for me for now. And I appreciate your kindness."

"Then, let's do this. How much time will you need in here?"

"I can be ready in ten minutes."

"I'll see you outside in eight, then."

She chuckles and I make my exit as loudly as I can, being sure to say goodbye to the remaining staff before heading out, even though I'd never done such a thing before.

My hands are shaking by the time I make it to my car, but I'm able to do what needs to be done.

"You ready?" I ask when she steps out the emergency exit door with a duffle over her shoulder. The hoodie does nothing to disguise her. Anyone would be able to tell it's her. But I do appreciate the effort she's made to be incognito.

"You ready to see my house, your new home?"

"Absolutely." She climbs into the passenger seat, looking to me with eyes that see her knight in shining armor, and then we go.

CHAPTER TWELVE

The exterior of the house is dark as we arrive, which is what I wanted. Pulling into the garage, I close the door right away so Tula can remain unseen.

As we make our way inside, the darkness follows. I keep the lights off. I take Tula by the hand and lead her down the hallway to the door at the end. I open it for her, wait for her to enter, and then swiftly close it behind her. The locking mechanisms engage, one after the other, echoing throughout the walls and up to the rafters before a silence heavy as death falls in the wake.

I can't hear anything from her through all the soundproofing.

Willing my adrenaline-filled heart to slow down, I enter the room adjacent, pulling a large oil painting from the wall, revealing a two-way mirror that allows me to see her. Clicking on the small light, I can see she is standing in the center of the room, startled by the sudden flicker of the bulb. She spins and I see the hope drain from her face when she sees she has no exit.

Its just her and the chair in there. The chair I took from the evidence room where it has been sitting for years. Having caught a serial creep a few years ago who built contraptions such as this for his hobbies—hobbies including the kidnapping and rape of women.

The chair is thick wood, handcrafted to fit hidden metal cuffs at the wrist and ankle spots. They are triggered as a unit after all four sensors are set simultaneously. It won't activate until the person, in this case, Tula, sits in a position where her ankles and wrists rest snuggly against the correct spots.

Then, like an animal trap, it snaps quickly around the limbs, shackling the victim to the chair. Once that's done, I will be able to bring chains in and hoist her into a more ideal position. One that leaves her tightly secure and immobile.

I don't know how long it will take her to activate the chair, I don't know enough about her to know if she even gets tired and needs to sit. But I have time to wait and I know she can't get out of this room whether she gets bolted down or not. The walls are reenforced, and no amount of otherworldly strength could break through, that is, if she were to possess any such thing. I can't imagine a come-guzzler needs that kind of strength, but I don't know anything in detail about her. I'm banking mostly on my comic book collection, and none of them are like Tula.

***

I'm surprised when it takes almost a week before she even sits in the chair. Mostly, she stood, arms crossed, staring at the mirror as though she were trying to ignite it, sometimes not moving from the position for hours. But then it happens. I don't know if its exhaustion or surrender that puts her ass in the seat, but whatever it was, thank fuck for it.

Looking back on the feed, I see her slump into it and in less than twenty minutes she's triggered the chair. A loud snapping as all four of the claws close tightly with her inside them.

She yelps, tugging instinctively against them to no avail. As I stand and watch her now, she seems resigned to simply stare at the mirror again. I watch the rise and fall of her chest as the only thing she does now is breathe and blink.

I leave her be for more days, she has told me that she can go without sustenance for longer than my entire life and not die. I need her at least weakened by lack of nourishment before I risk my neck in there with her. So, for now, patience is my friend.

***

On the day that I feel brave enough to deal with her, stealing myself at the door before going inside, excitement is abundant.

Her eyes land on me, and instead of looking away, I stare back into hers so she knows I'm not going to back down.

"Bradley," she starts, her voice scratchy and hoarse. She pauses briefly, clearing her throat before starting again. "You don't have to do this." Her eyes bore into mine, pleading for her release since her words aren't working.

"Don't I, Tula? I'm not a bad man. But sometimes good men do things like this because they *need* to. Because something in them *drives* them to it. In all my police years I've seen men be driven to do some of the most bizarre shit and all because of a woman. You can't tell me I don't *need* to do this. It's in our nature to do *exactly* this. Go after, and take, what you want. Stop at *nothing* to get what you want. I have never wanted anything as much as you. There was nothing that could get in the way. Not even you."

"I would have been yours."

"For a time, I'm sure that's true. But I couldn't risk you not being here when I needed it. It's not like I could go out and find another of you, or even the next best thing. What you have is the most mind-altering drug and I couldn't risk not having it."

A tear falls down her cheek then disappears into her skin. She shakes her head, but doesn't say another word.

I take her silence as permission to carry on with what I was doing. And that means dragging the chains in here to get her up and ready to fuck.

***

Once she is secured in the shackles, arms above her head, elbows firmly pressed against her ears. Each of her legs double manacled tightly to the wall. It would take a locksmith along with a good-sized army to free her from this.

I begin setting up the room for her long-term stay. There is a cage of rot iron in the closet that I wheel out and lock into place with anchors built into the floor. It's just large enough to fit around her, making her look very much like a bird. It has several doors and removable sections so I can access any part of her safely whenever I want to.

She has the look of pure hellfire in her eyes as I hoist and maneuver her into position with the chain pulley system. It makes me a little uneasy, only because I don't know the scope of her abilities or strength. If she's lived as long as the earth, she may have some evolutionary badassery in there I know nothing about.

But at least I know that all this steel is here to counter any surprises—surely, she's not stronger than good ol' American steel.

I can't help but watch her, naked now and completely restrained. Something about her like this making it all the more erotic.

There is a part of me that knows I should wait longer, she's mine now, and I have all the time in the world to use her, but it's been so long already and I'm sure it wouldn't be catastrophic if I just get the head in.

My fingers slide along her pussy, she's dryer than normal and I assume it's from dehydration. She's still warm down there and that's all I need right now anyway.

I angle my cock into her, the sensations nearly do me in that instant. But I'm able to push it a little more, getting my entire head in and out before frantically scrambling away from her and exploding. I'm sure not to leave anything behind.

Her tongue darts out and I know she's hungry for it, but I know I can't feed her.

Without a word, I leave the room and hang the painting back up; I have no desire to stand and watch her like this.

Knowing that she is mine now, and having just had a release, I'm finally able to relax. The weight of addiction lifted; I am once again in control.

Making food and getting some phone calls into the station is a breeze when you've finally gotten things taken care of.

***

That night, sleep was peaceful, I awoke only once to check on Tula. She was unmoving, I waited to see her chest rise and fall to be sure she wasn't dead, then I went back to sleep.

I worked my shift and returned home, checked on Tula, who was fuming again.

I waited a painful two weeks, while sticking to this routine, before I initiated contact with her next. I needed her to be tired and hungry, but mostly I needed her to have given up hope.

The door creeks a little when it's opened, which alerts Tula's to my arrival.

She has her red-rimmed eyes on me when I flip on the light.

"Bradley?" Confusion, along with betrayal, hint in her question.

I feel a little tug of sadness for her. She seems so small in here. No remorse or regret, though. I did what I had to do.

"What are you doing with me?"

"Keeping you."

"Why like this?"

"I suppose, this is how I wanted you."

"I liked you."

"I know that. But I couldn't be the chief who's always inside a strip club, the town would start to talk. I couldn't be seen with you or my reputation would be ruined."

"You did this to save face?"

"I suppose that sums it up."

"Your species really has *no* redeeming qualities." Her expression turns to one of hatred, squinting at me with the anger she feels for all of mankind. It's enough that I finally have to look away.

She may be right.

Opening the latch, I pull the cage away. Checking the locks on her extremities and collaring the last one around her neck, carefully so as not to choke her.

When I set up this room, I had it fitted with a hose to clean the tiled floor of her bodily mess, it seems that she must use all of it for food because there is no sign of any waste, not even the hint of urine, she either doesn't have that function, or is not creating waste for now, either way, it's a win for me.

"I wish you'd change your mind about all of this. It's not necessary."

"I wish you'd stop begging. I do have a gag if I feel it might help with that."

"Fine, but when you're done with me, can I go back to my life?"

"I don't see why not."

She quiets her inquiry and I approach her again, tugging my pants off.

My cock is more than ready to be inside of her. I jacked off a few hours ago so I wouldn't be so eager that I make a mistake and accidently come inside of her—to death.

Her hole is so warm. All the sensations I crave overtake me, sending a shiver of ecstasy down my spine. I hold off long enough to get a full minute inside of her before clumsily dragging myself away and coming into a container I can take with me as I go.

"Could I have that?" she asks, hopeful.

"Not yet. I'm sorry."

"So, you plan on leaving me in here to starve for an undetermined amount of time? Just so I'm clear."

"Yes."

"You are the worst of them."

"I might be." I leave her with that, reinforcing her cage before I go.

CHAPTER THIRTEEN

It's a full two years before I decide introduce Keith to Tula. I thought I'd be nice and let him in on the little secret I have hidden in my house. Best friends, and all. So, one night I invite him over, knowing he'd be excited for Tula as much as I always am.

"You want to see what I've been up to?" I say when he walks into the living room, freshly opened beer in his hand.

"You've been up to something?"

"Yea, fucker. You wanna see, or you wanna go fuck yourself?"

"Those the only options? I guess I *could* fuck myself," he jokes.

"I've got something that could do that for you."

"If you're hinting at some gay shit, I'm not interested—unless... nope I'm interested," he says, laughing. "You got a woman?" he asks after some thought.

Growing up together and having the same taste in women lent us to a lot of 'wrong' kind of threesomes.

"There is a lady."

He looks almost like I've told him the most shocking thing ever.

"*You* have a lady?"

"I do."

"And she wants a piece of me?"

"Well..."

Reading my evasiveness, he says, "Ok, I take it this is going to be a more *show* than *tell* kind of thing since you are being super vague, for someone who is sharing something."

"It's hard to explain. But you're going to *love* it."

"Lead the way, my friend, I'm always ready for one of your stunts."

I unlock the door to Tula instead of showing her off through the two-way mirror. I feel the impact is much better this way.

I have him enter first, and then hit the light, his jaw drops the instant he sees her.

She's a little thinner then when I took her in. Discovering that if I give her only a drop or two of my come every other day or so, it leaves her looking her best, and also feeling her best, without all the pesky side effects of actual strength or mental fortitude. She's as docile as euthanized cat.

I also learned that starvation dries her up. So, if only for my own selfishness and lubrication, I give her food.

He looks at me a full minute, mouth agape, before saying anything.

"This is the stripper that went missing years ago. You've had her this whole time?"

"I have."

"And you've kept her chained up in here, *naked*, like some fucking sex slave?"

"Yes. I suppose if you want it all the way to the bare bones, I have done that."

"Holy fuck! You're a genius."

"So, you want in?"

"*Fuck* yes! I want in that." He unbuttons his pants but I stop him before he can continue.

"You *can't* finish in her. You have to use the cup. She'll suck you dry 'til you die."

"No shit? Could be the way I'd welcome death," he says, and then contemplates it momentarily, rubbing the scruff on his chin.

"Seriously, she's some sort of creature."

He mockingly winks at me. "Got it."

"Seriously. Put your dick in her, then when you feel it pulling and you're on the verge of coming, you *need* to pull out."

"Fine." Keith takes his dick out, and for the purpose of helping him survive, I stay to supervise.

He reaches between her legs, she flinches, but doesn't speak, she gave up talking to me over a year ago.

I move the lower section of the cage away and let him get closer. "Go ahead."

He slips inside of her and I can see his face, the face I must have had when I was introduced to the best feeling in the world.

Eight seconds is all it takes for him to get that look in his eyes that says I need to pull him out.

He spirts into the container I am unfortunately holding at the time and then flops to the floor, twitching a little.

I give him a few minutes to feel better, but when he is clearly not recovered, I take a turn with Tula. I have gotten to where I can actually fuck her, which makes it all feel so much more intense.

If someone had told me it could get better than in the beginning, I'd have called them a fucking liar. But it's true, the sensation multiplies, feeling like my soul is being sucked through my cock.

My dick swells and her pussy pulls me back into her, milking me to the point of lightheadedness. Then I press myself entirely into her and let all the magic happen, every bit of her pussy tugs and rubs my cock until I'm one second from releasing, at which point, I finally drag myself out of her and unload in the container on top of Keith's deposit.

Fourteen minutes is my record. Practicing multiple times, a day helps build a tolerance.

He's on his feet when I finish, watching in awe at what I've been able to accomplish, what he has to think, is the impossible.

"Shit dude. That's intense."

"I know." I engage the cage and usher him out the door.

"So, you're serious about not coming in her. She is something else, huh?"

"Yea, she's a fucking sex machine," I laugh. Still unsure whether I'll get into her origin story for him. It's not necessary, and it doesn't really matter, he'll follow the rules if he wants inside of her again.

"So, when's it my turn again?"

"At first, I'm going to have to help you, like I did today."

"Oh, yea, for sure, there was no way I was pulling out of that."

"But after I get you trained, she's all yours whenever you want. I'll give you a key."

"You know, in school when everyone was saying you were such a loser, I guess they were wrong."

"No one said I was a loser in school."

"But if they had, they'd be wrong."

"You're such a douche."

"Let's fucking eat something. I'm starving."

***

It took Keith much longer to get the hang of pulling out of Tula than I thought it would. At least he's quick about fucking her, less than a minute and no sign of being able to last any longer. Three months, fucking her daily at least once, with little to no progress.

If he weren't my best friend, I'd get annoyed with all the babysitting. But I can understand what she does. That hole is magic, so I forgive, even though he doesn't seem embarrassed, or apologetic for that matter, that he's still unable to accomplish it solo.

***

After the six-month mark, he's been on his own. When he was finally able to make it a full month of pulling out successfully, and using the container for his deposit, I gave him a key. I suppose if he dies, he dies. He knows the risks and is well aware of the dire consequences.

CHAPTER FOURTEEN

TULA

On a random day, nearly eight years into my entrapment, I find hope.

Keith has spoken to me. He'd never said anything, just as Bradley had instructed him. But today, he talks. It's only to tell me that he's going to fuck the shit out of me. But it says something to me about him. It tells me he likes dirty talk.

I'm weakened by the lack of nutrition. Not so much that death is near, but enough to notice. And on top of eight years near starvation, I'd been eating only the simplest diet for thousands, keeping me from my peak as it were. It was a decision I didn't know would have such a severe penalty.

Keith fucks me, grunting and thrusting, I give him the smallest whimper. And it sets him off.

Men are all the same.

He empties outside of me, into the cup that makes me salivate.

"Did you like that?" he asks, his face close to mine, blowing heavy bursts of cigarette scented breath at me.

I nod, coyly, looking at him through my eyelashes.

He looks elated that I've been sexually gratified. Not sure what to expect from him, I nearly laugh when he thinks the best course of action is to shove his fingers into me and give me more of the 'good stuff'. Maybe he thinks I'll like it, so I do—for him.

He thrusts them in and out of me, in a way that can only be described as chaotic, while I give him my best fuck-me eyes.

He squeezes my nipple too hard, but I make him think he's doing a good job. Another moan, and then a shutter that hopefully appears to him as though I've orgasmed. Thankfully, it does make him stop. There's a cheesy grin on his face, satisfied in his own efforts to please me.

He pulls his fingers from me, "Did you like that?"

"Yes." My voice hasn't been used in so long I'd forgotten it myself. The tickle of it in my throat almost makes me cough.

"Good." Reengaging the lock to my cage quickly, he leaves.

***

A full year later the relationship is getting strong with Keith. One he's obviously keeping from Bradley.

We talk, and he does his best to please me sexually. As if that could possibly be what I might need in my current situation.

But I'm trying. And for now, it's at least keeping my mind fresh and hopeful.

Bradley uses me for what he wants and nothing more. Feeding me miniscule amounts, I'm convinced it's only to keep me looking good for him.

His need for me is ever increasing. He fucks me five times a day on average. While Keith has only gotten the ability to see me twice a day, sometimes only to talk and finger me. It's almost worse than Bradley, Keith thinks he's a good guy because he humanizes me. At least with Bradley, I'm just a hole, not much humanity needed for a hole.

If I were a regular woman, my pussy would probably not withstand this schedule. At no other time, in my infinitely long life, am I more grateful to be me.

This will be a mere blip in my lifespan, my mind will not even remember it soon enough. What will linger is the memories of what *I* do to *them*.

***

Keith walks in, cock already swollen, and is quick to get inside of me.

As I've done with him for a while, I moan and beg him for more, fucking him back as best I can within my limits, making him eager to please me.

"Oh god, Keith, don't stop. You feel so good. Make me come. Let me show you what my pussy does to your cock when you make me come. The pleasure you will feel when it floods for you and trickles to the floor, the tightness will give you more ecstasy than you've ever imagined."

Anything I can think of to make him finish.

He grumbles and grunts, pushing his dick to the limits, and this time, I've got him, the rush of my dirty words in his ear sends him somewhere else, somewhere where he can be free.

That little, salty bead starts forming, hunger and instinct start pulling and sucking on his seed.

He hesitates, and I can tell he wants to retreat, but I don't let him. I squeeze him tightly inside me and watch as he quickly surrenders himself to the fate of being my nourishment. All for those few moments of rapture. Emptying inside of me, I watch his head lull back as I milk him dry, devouring his life force, giving me strength.

His cock shrivels inside of me as I take everything from him, my hunger getting the best of me. I drain him completely, and it's been a long time since I've done that.

Keith flops forward, his head landing on my chest, my mouth salivates, my teeth start to ache, something I haven't felt in hundreds of years.

My jaw separates instinctually to make room for the rest of my meal. The raw energy revitalizing my primal form. It's been so long since I've been my true self.

Rows of jagged teeth push through my gums. My mouth salivates, eager to taste him. The adjacent rows of incisors begin to gnaw back and forth. Stretching my face to accommodate whatever part of his body I choose first. Replaying his disgusting moans and nauseating words in my mind as I go straight for his face. Grinding up the meat and crushing the bones that give it structure. Before long, I've made my way to his brain, delicious as caviar to me. And when it's gone, I finish the meal by sucking every bit of his spinal fluid through his exposed brain stem.

I feel my strength return completely, my real strength, giving me enough to tear my arms free, then an unsteady and shaky leg hits the cool floor.

I take his hand into my mouth, shoving it deeper as I grind and crunch hungrily. Blood splatters across the walls of my confined space. Meat comes away and slides down my esophagus until I reach his shoulder. Slurping on it as I pull only the thickest part of bones back out.

Each pound of flesh reminds me how delicious humans can really be, and by the time I've consumed him completely, leaving the heart to eat last, savoring the final beat of it against my tongue, I'm free, and only just getting started.

***

Based on Bradley's routine I expect he will be home soon. Sitting on the couch, covered in blood, but back to the form he'll recognize, I wait.

The door creaks, tugging a little smile on my lips. He's not nearly as stunned as he should be when our eyes meet.

He pauses at the open door of my blood-soaked prison and sees Keith on the floor, nothing but random bones, I'm sure he has questions, but he asks none.

I can hear his heart thundering inside his chest, so I know it has affected him.

"Surprised to see me, Bradley?"

No response.

I stand, making my way toward him. Every step I take, he retreats one, keeping us the same distance apart until his back is against the wall.

I say nothing, licking his friend's blood from my mouth.

Bradley stammers, starting multiple times before finally being able to finish a sentence. "What the fuck, Tula, you don't have to do this. I got crazy with lust, I just wanted you so much. I can do better, I'll let you out, you can be free. We can be together."

"Shut up, Bradley, I've heard you speak enough." I cut off his rambling by wrapping my fingers snugly around his throat. "You're about to see me, the real me, I think it's only fair, you've shown me your monster, now I'll show you mine. Although, I have to say mine is not intended to be malicious or self-serving, mine is for the health and well-being of the earth—her balance. Not nearly as callus as yours.

"I'm an eradicator of creators, a good to an evil, a yin to a yang, a destroyer of parasites. Taking the form of earth's biggest threats, and preventing them from taking more than she wants to give.

"I've been so many things over the ages. Humans had fascinated me with their ability to understand and express beyond all other things before them. I suppose, I'd fallen in love with them, I didn't want to remove them, maybe I even wanted to be one, hence my need to find an alternate way to feed. But the novelty is wearing off because of selfish takers like you and Keith. What you have done has filled me with hate. Which I have only ever experienced as a human. So many new emotions in this form. Can you imagine what my life was like being an invasive algae or a beetle, not much emotion.

"Recently, I have had so much time to think about it and reflect. Having myself removed, gave me time to *really* see. And do you know what I realized? Through my hazy love-filled eyes, I was looking passed all the *horrible* things your species does, not only to the earth, but to each other. You don't love, you only envy. You don't care, only cultivate, you hate on many levels, everyone, for everything. The earth has been *begging* for me to help her."

I don't let him speak, my hand remains around his throat, only to keep him from running.

"My saliva is a numbing agent. It doesn't mean you can't feel anything, it just means your brain won't know that you're in pain. The side effect of that is it won't tell you to die, it just keeps going."

I disengage my jaw, and he watches, in horror, as my teeth come out. Row after row emerge and start to ungulate back and forth, ready to grind and crush.

His scream awakens a laugh so guttural I feel it in my bones. Then he tries to run and it excites me.

Taking his arm and shoving it into my mouth brings about his primal panic, a sight I have missed. The next arm slurps out of my mouth and he stands with his boney appendages at his sides, trickling blood onto the carpeted floor.

He tries to catch himself when I knock him to the ground but his stubby, kickstand bones crumple under his weight. I tear his pants off, and I see the disgusting twitch of his dick as it starts to respond in the only way it can in my presence. Hoping, even as I stand in this terrifying form, he may have one last opportunity to feel me and plant his seed to grow inside me like the parasite it would be.

The hope is gone when his foot enters my mouth, the spray of blood hits my face, but I'm able to catch the rest as I make my way higher up to his thigh until the meat is gone. The round belly I've not had in so long is welcome, I'd forgotten the bliss of fullness.

Having tossed his cock to the side, making sure I'd never have that maggot inside of me again, I eat around his remaining torso and head, leaving his eyes, brain, and heart for last, in the hopes that he can see, process, and feel his annihilation.

I show him just who out monsters whom, when I force him to watch me, in human form, with a smile across my face, eat his still-beating heart, and finally, I pop each of his eyes into my mouth, one at a time. Savoring the delicious fear inside of him before I devour all that he ever experienced in his brain.

If he's taught me anything, it's that this entire race is built with primitive selfishness, arrogance, and consumption. A revolting organism, and I may just have to exterminate them all.

The end

Thank you for reading

More by Rayne

Boys Will Be Boys

Tantalize

The Other Place

Killstreme

Daddy Issues

Collecting Rayne Vol 1
includes

My Christmas Story

The Boy

Degenerate

Devour

Retaliation

XXX

app

The Embalmer

Made in the USA
Columbia, SC
12 March 2023